The Baby's Game Book

Selected by
ISABEL WILNER

Pictures by
SAM WILLIAMS

Greenwillow Books
An Imprint of HarperCollinsPublishers

Pencil and watercolors were used for the full-color art.
The text type is Novarese.

The Baby's Game Book
Compilation copyright © 2000 by Isabel Wilner
Illustrations copyright © 2000 by Sam Williams
Printed in Singapore by Tien Wah Press. All rights reserved.
http://www.harperchildrens.com

Library of Congress Cataloging-in-Publication Data

Wilner, Isabel.
The baby's game book / Isabel Wilner ;
pictures by Sam Williams.
p.   cm.
"Greenwillow Books."
Summary: Rhymes, illustrations, and instructions
present a variety of simple games to play with babies, including foot
tapping, knee rides, finger play, peek-a-boo, and tickle games.
ISBN 0-688-15916-8
1. Games—Juvenile literature.   [1. Finger play.   2. Games.
3. Nursery rhymes.]   I. Williams, Sam, ill.
II. Title.   GV1203.W68   2000   649'.5—dc21
98-22120   CIP   AC

3 4 5 6 7 8 9 10   First Edition

For
Debby Amoss
—I. W.

For
the Beeds!
—S. W.

A NOTE TO PLAYERS

You may remember some of these games from your own childhood. Although some have instructions and others have picture clues, there is no one right way to play a game with a baby. The most important thing is to touch, talk, and have fun!

AUTHOR'S NOTE

◆ Hold your baby in your lap or place your baby in front of you in a sit-up seat. Look into your baby's eyes. Now bring your baby's hands together inside your own and chant, "Pat-a-cake, pat-a-cake, baker's man. . . ." You've just played a game. It may not be Crazy Eights or Giant Steps, but it's a game all right, one that builds a foundation as rock solid and rewarding as any in the world.

◆ Combining physical play and word play, games like Pat-a-Cake and the others described here foster the development of rhythm. The rhythm required for complex movements as disparate as dancing or swinging a baseball bat begins in these early efforts to use arms and legs in an organized, meaningful fashion. And these games also instill in developing infants and toddlers an effortless ease with words and word combinations. No skill will serve them better later, when they learn to read. They'll know right from the start, through play, that sounds are words, that words have meaning, that meaning brings joy.

◆ But the most critical benefit of traditional games like Pat-a-Cake surpasses any quantitative justification. No vessel exists big enough to measure the depth of understanding and commitment forged between adult and child as the two of you indulge in the pure pleasure of play in its most elemental form. The head and the heart work in tandem, and memories are made that last a lifetime.

Isabel Wilner

PEEK-A-BOO

(Cover and uncover your face with your hands)

Where's the baby?
Peek-a-boo!
There's the baby.
I see you!

Bath Game

(As you wash the baby)

Rub-a-dub-dub,
Give the baby a scrub
With soap and water
In a nice clean tub.

Foot Tapping

(Pat the baby's bare feet)

Shoe a little horse.
Shoe a little mare.
But let the little colt
Go bare, bare, bare.

Foot Tapping

(Pat the baby's bare feet)

Pitty, patty, polt.
Shoe the wild colt.
Here a nail,
And there a nail.
Pitty, patty, polt.

Foot Game

(Move the baby's legs up and down)

See-saw, sacradown.
This is the way
to London Town.

One foot up and
the other down.
And that is the way
to London Town.

Knee Ride

(The baby sits on your knees, facing you)

This is the way the ladies ride.

Pace, pace, pace, pace, pace.

(Knees move gently up and down)

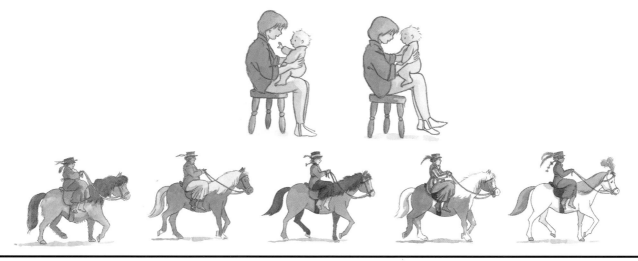

This is the way the gentlemen ride.

Gallop-a-trot, gallop-a-trot, gallop-a-trot.

(Knees move faster)

This is the way the farmer men ride.

Hobble-de-hoy, hobble-de-hoy,

(Move first one knee and then the other to give the baby a bumpy ride)

hobble-de-hoy.

Knee Ride

To market, to market
To buy a fat pig.
Home again, home again,
Jiggety-jig.

To market, to market
To buy a fat hog.
Home again, home again,
Jiggety-jog.

Knee Ride

To market, to market
To buy a plum cake.
Back again, back again,
Baby is late.

To market, to market
To buy a plum bun.
Back again, back again,
Market is done.

Knee Ride

(The baby sits on your knees, facing you)

Come along, my little pony.
A-cantering we'll go.
Trot, trot, tappity-trot,
Trot, trot, tappity-trot,
Trot, trot, tappity-trot,
Trot, trot, WHOA!

Come along, my little pony,
A-galloping we'll go.
Tap, tap, tappety-tap,
Tappety, tappety, tappety-tap,
Tap, tap, tappety-tap,
Tappety, tappety, WHOA!

18

Knee Ride

(Bounce the baby on your knee)

Trot, trot, trot.

Go and never stop.

Trudge along, my little pony,

Where it's rough and where it's stony.

Go and never stop.

Trot, trot, trot, trot, trot!

Leg over leg,
As the dog went to Dover.
When he came to a stile—
JUMP! He went over.

(Cross your knees and sit the baby on one ankle, holding the baby's hands. Bounce the baby to the rhythm of the rhyme and on "JUMP" give the baby a big swing by uncrossing your knees)

(The baby sits on your knees, facing you. You hold the baby's hands. Say:)

Fall-y,

Fall-y,

Fall-y,

Fall-y,

And UP again!

(Slowly let the baby down, then pull the baby up quickly)

Fingers

Master Thumb is first to come,
Then Pointer, steady and strong,
Then Tall Man high,
And just nearby
The Feeble Man does linger.
And last of all,
So neat and small,
Comes Little Pinky Finger.

Naming the Fingers

Thumb bold

Tibbity-told

Longman

Lick pan

Little little little man

Thumb bold,
Tibbity-told,
Longman,
Lick pan,
Little little little man.

23

Finger Game

(*Start with the thumb. At the end,
tickle the baby's little finger and
then tickle up the baby's arm*)

This
little
cow
eats
grass.

This
little
cow
eats
hay.

This
little
cow
drinks
water.

This little
cow runs
away.

This little cow
does nothing—
But just lies
down all day.

We'll chase her, we'll chase her, we'll chase her away!

Hand Clapping

Pat-a-cake,

Pat-a-cake,

Baker's man,

Bake me a cake

As fast as you can.

Pat it and prick it

And mark it with B,

And put it in the oven

For Baby and me.

Pat it,
Kiss it,
Stroke it,
Bless it;
Three days sunshine,
Three days rain,
Little hand
All well
Again.

Finger Game

(Hold your fist in such a way that if the baby puts a finger in, you can secure it)

Put your finger in Foxy's den. Foxy's not at home.
Foxy's at the back door, picking on a bone.

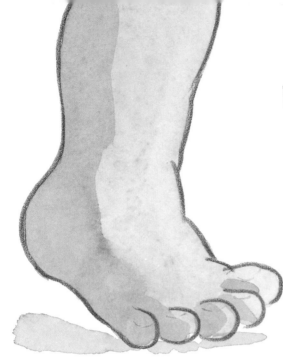

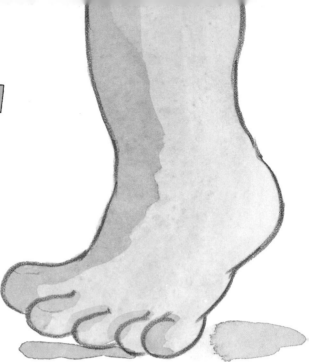

Naming the Toes

(Start with the little toe)

Wee wiggie,
Poke piggie,
Tom Whistle,
John Gristle,
And old big
GOBBLE
Gobble
Gobble!

Wee wiggie Poke piggie Tom Whistle John Gristle GOBBLE

29

Naming the Toes

(Start with the big toe)

Harry Whistle,
Tommy Thistle,
Willy Whible,
Johnny Thible,
And Little Oker Bell.

(Start with the big toe)

This little pig went to market.
This little pig stayed home.
This little pig had roast beef.
This little pig had none.
This little pig cried "Wee wee wee"
All the way home.

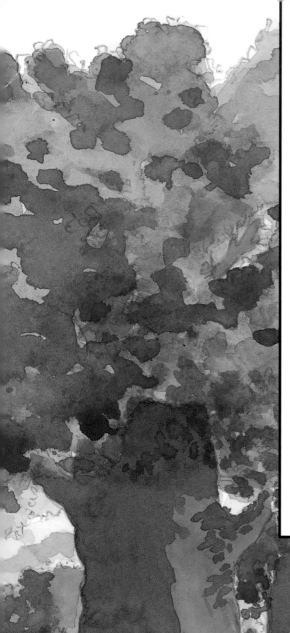
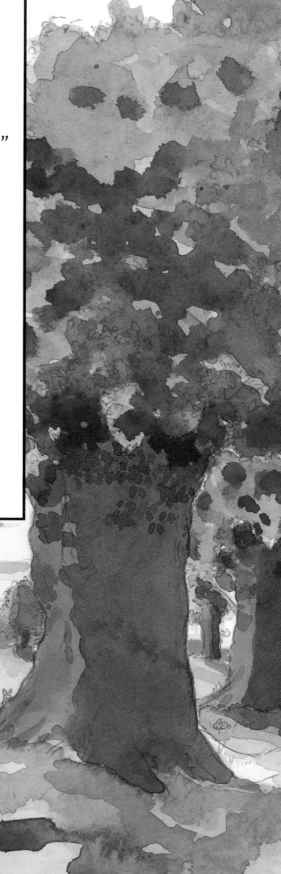

Toe Game

(Start with the little toe)

"Let's go to the wood,"
    says this pig.
"What to do there?"
    says that pig.
"To look for my mother,"
    says this pig.
"What to do with her?"
    says that pig.
"To kiss her, to kiss her,"
    says this pig.

Face Game

(*Point to the baby's features*)

Two little eyes
to look around,
Two little ears
to hear each sound,
One little nose
to smell what's sweet,
One little mouth
that likes to eat.

33

(Point to the baby's features)

Here sits Farmer Giles.
(forehead)

Here sit his two men.
(eyes)

Here sits the cock.
(cheek)

Here sits the hen.
(cheek)

Here sit the chickens.
(nose)

Here they run in.
(mouth)

Chin chopper, Chin chopper, Chin chopper, CHIN.

Round and round the garden

(Run your index finger around the baby's palm)

Went the Teddy Bear.

One step,

Two steps,

(Jump your finger up the baby's arm)

Tickly under there.

(Tickle under the baby's arm)

*(Tapping begins with the baby's toes and ends
with tickles over the head and down the back)*

Toe-sy woe-sy,

Wee footy,

Shin chappy,

Knee nappy,

Bulgie wulgie,

Neckie peckie,

Chinny winny,

Mouthie southie,

Nosy posy,

Eye winky,

Brow brinky,

Over the crown,

Down we go,

Down, down, down.

38

Tickle Game

Round the world!
Round the world!
Catch a big bear.
Where are we going
to catch him?
Right in
THERE!

(Draw a big circle in the air around the baby, and make the circle smaller and smaller until it reaches the baby's belly button)

39

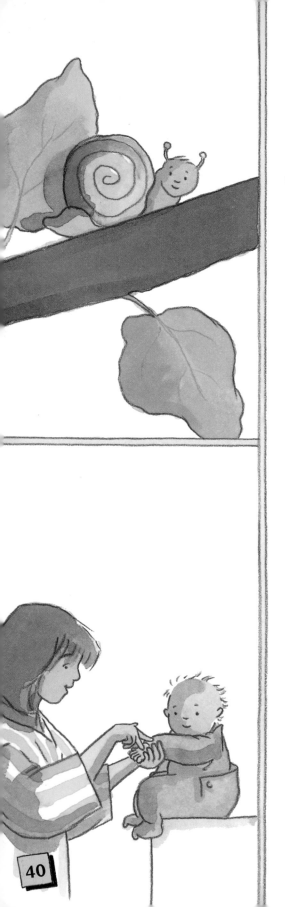

Tickle Game

(Move your fingers slowly up baby's arm and body. Then do it again—very quickly)

Slowly, slowly, very slowly
Creeps the garden snail.
Slowly, slowly, very slowly
Up the wooden rail.
Quickly, quickly, very quickly
Runs the little mouse.
Quickly, quickly, very quickly
Round about the house.

How to Make Raisin Bread

(Put the baby on the bed or floor, then roll the baby back and forth)

You roll it,
You roll it,
You roll it,
You roll it,
And then you put
the raisins in!

(Give little pokes all over the baby)

Counting Game

How many days

1 Saturday

4 Tuesday

5 Wednesday

8 Saturday

9 Sunday

2 Sunday

3 Monday

6 Thursday

7 Friday

10 Monday

has my
baby
to play?

43

The Love Game

(This is a game for two players whose two hands measure their love. Say:)

I love you this much

(holding hands slightly apart)

I love you this much

I love you this much

(making the space between hands larger)
The game continues until the stretching has reached its limit.

Good Morning

Baby, baby, open your eye,
For the sun is in the sky;
And he's peeping
once again
Through the clear, bright
window pane;
Little baby, do not keep
Any longer fast asleep.

Bedtime

Give baby a hug,
Give baby a kiss.
Toss baby into beddie-bye
Just like this.

INDEX OF FIRST LINES